Santa's Hat

By Allan Brookdale

For My Girls,
Carllene, and Maddy
with all my love
Dad

Nearly every little boy and every little girl can tell you the story of Santa Claus. The stories may be a little different depending on which part of the world in which you live, but basically, they're all the same. This story is about something that happened to jolly old St. Nick. Something that almost kept Christmas away one year, something that sent the elves running in a panic. Something so horrible that Mrs. Claus came close to having a hoozy-doozy fit. This story is about the time that Santa lost his hat. Oh, I know what you're thinking: Lost his hat- big deal! You've probably lost a hat or two in your day. But you've never had a hat like this one. This hat was like no other on earth. And for a time, this hat was lost. Sort of. Let me begin.

Our story starts early in the morning on December 23rd. The day-before-the-day-before-Christmas...

One

A light, and gentle snow fell in the night. The thick and fluffy snowflakes adding yet another soft, white layer to the already snow-covered North Pole. All was well. That was outside. Inside, deep in the heart of Christmas Castle, trouble was already tiptoeing across the floor. Santa didn't know it yet, but he was just about to find out.

Santa's eyes popped open with a start and his heart pounded away deep within his large chest. Sweat stood out on the pointy ends of his frosty white eyebrows.

"Oh, my." He said quietly, taking a deep breath. "What a dream." He reached up and stroked his long, white beard. "A very, very scary dream." But he couldn't really remember what it was about. He reached over to the nightstand next to his side of the bed and picked up his glasses. Perching them on the tip of his nose he stared at Father Time's old clock across the room.

"Goodness me," Santa said reading the time, "It's just half past three in the morning, much too early. Much, much too early indeed." He snuck a peek at Mrs. Claus who lay snuggled up under the blankets softly snoring out of her cute little nose. "I must go back to sleep." Santa mumbled. "I've much to do and not much time in which to do it. I need to rest." He fluffed up his pillow and settled back down to sleep.

"Much to do…" His eyelids slowly closed, and he was just drifting off when he remembered the dream. Santa sat up so quickly that this time Mrs. Claus awoke.

"Are you all right dear?' She asked yawning.

"Something's wrong." Santa said whispered.

"Well, what is it?" Mrs. Claus asked, still not quite awake.

"I don't think I know." Santa said as he slowly slid out of bed. He was wearing a long red nightshirt with silver buttons on the front. Little red socks with pointy little tips covered his feet. He stood, listening very closely. Tick-tock, tick-tock. The old clock was the only sound. "Something just feels wrong." He said.

Quick as a rabbit he jumped for the bedroom door. One, two, three giant steps and he slid across the wood floor. He flung open the door and stood looking out into the great hall.

Little groups of small elves were spread across the room working away at this and that. One was putting together tiny toy cars that *vroom-vroomed* when you rolled them on the floor.

Another was busy dressing tiny dolls so they could drive the little toy cars. One group just sat on the floor drinking hot chocolate not doing much of anything.

When I say they were small elves I mean s-s-s-m-m-m-a-a-a-a-l-l-l. These little guys and little girls were the tiniest of all elves, barely there at all.

Well, when their boss, Santa, threw the door open all of the elves stopped what they were doing and stared. The tiniest of all the elves pointed at Santa's red nightshirt with the silver buttons and giggled. Santa gave her a stern look indeed. The tiny elf clasped her hands over her mouth to keep from laughing but then the pointy tips of her ears turned bright red and started to wiggle back and forth. Santa raised an eyebrow and gave her an even harder look. Some of the other elves rushed over and tried to keep her from laughing but they were too late. First, a tiny, little giggle slipped out from between her fingers. Next, a "he-he-he", tumbled out followed by a full-out laugh. "Ha-ha-ha-ha-ha!" Santa quickly smiled, his eyes twinkled, and he let out his famous deep, barrel-chested laugh.

"Ho, ho, ho! Don't you worry little ones," He said, "I guess I must be a funny site to you indeed. Ho, ho, ho!"
All at once all of the elves started laughing and slapping each other on the back. The tiniest of all the elves rolled on the floor holding her stomach and laughed and laughed.

Santa slowly closed the bedroom door. Shaking his head, he started back across the room to his bed, the dream all but forgotten.

Then, all at once he stopped. The feeling that something was wrong was stronger than ever.

Mrs. Claus sat quietly in bed blinking in the dim light. She watched as Santa stood in the middle of the room his hands stroking his long beard. She could see he was really thinking hard.

Suddenly Santa leaped from where he was standing and one, two, three steps slid over to the closet door. For an old guy Santa is pretty speedy. He opened the door and quick-as-a-lick flicked on the light.

Hanging on one side of the closet were Mrs. Claus's pretty red dresses. All sixty-two of them, each one the same, all lined up nice and neat.

On the other side hung Santa's red pants, white shirts, and red jackets. Also, all lined up nice and neat. Beneath those sat his shiny black boots all in a row.

At the end of the long closet up against the back wall, a crystal-clear case, the size of a large watermelon, sat on a heavy wooden table.

The crystal case was created to hold Santa's most prized possession, something so magical, so mystical that it had to have a special resting place to protect it; Santa's hat.

So, a very, very long time ago the elves of the Blue Ice Mountains pulled the crystal out of their deepest mine. They spent a hundred days hollowing, and cutting, and polishing the crystal until it was perfectly clear. Then they gave the crystal to Santa who placed it on the wooden table. Inside the crystal, the magic of the hat would never run out. Inside the crystal, the power of the hat would be safe for all-time. Inside the crystal- Santa gasped. He rushed up to the wooden table his hands trembling. Suddenly his eyes rolled back in his head, and he tumbled over backwards fainting away to land on the closet floor with a plop. Above Santa, on the table, and in the crystal, sat not the magical, mystical, all-powerful hat. Nope. There, pulled snug over the hat stand, was a red-and-white striped sock.

Two

Okay, so here we have Santa, the old guy himself, fainted away from the shock of seeing a red-and-white sock tucked all nice and tidy on the hat stand in the crystal case. Mrs. Claus, of course, rushed right over when she heard Santa fall with a plop on to his back. After much "oh my's" and a whole lot of "Oh dear's", she called the doctor and with the help of about a hundred of those tiny little elves I already mentioned got Santa into bed.

By the time Ezekial Coldhanz, Santa's private doctor, arrived the whole of Christmas Castle had heard the news: Santa's hat is missing, Santa fainted, and Santa wears a really funny looking red nightshirt to bed.

Ezekial Coldhanz put a stethoscope to Santa's chest and listened to Santa's heart a beat-beat-beating away.

"Sounds good to me." He said. He scratched his head. "I've never seen anything like this before in all my days." And Ezekial Coldhanz had been alive for over 600 years so he knew what he was talking about.

"You mean you've never seen someone faint before?" Mrs. Claus asked. Old Dr. Coldhanz scrunched up his nose, "No ma'am, I've seen that plenty of times." He pulled the blankets down a bit and pointed at Santa. "I've never seen such funny looking pajamas before." He shook his head, "Silver buttons and all."

"They were a gift," Mrs. Claus said, "From Cupid." The doctor looked at her even more strangely. "Hmmm. Well, anyways, I think he'll be just fine." He pulled the blankets back up around Santa's neck. "In fact, I'm sure of it. He'll probably sleep a little bit, then pop- he'll just wake up and be ready to go."

At that moment Santa's eyes flew open. He sat straight up in bed and looked around. Both Mrs. Claus and Dr. Coldhanz stared at him. The doctor was the first to speak.

"Ahem. See? There you are. Right as rain."
Santa looked at the good doctor as if he'd never seen him before. He looked at Mrs. Claus who looked pretty worried.

Santa leaned and looked over the side of the bed into the upturned and worried eyes of about a hundred tiny elves all bunched together. His face softened.

"Aw, you guys. I'm all right." He said to his workers. "I'm fine. Now back to work. We have much to do and not much time in which to do it." The elves started slowly filing out the door. "All right now. To work you guys." Santa encouraged.

The tiniest of elves turned as she reached the door.

"But Santa," she asked in a voice as small as small can be, "what about your hat?"

It was then that Santa remembered the missing hat. It was almost enough to make him faint again. He put his hand to his chest.

"Well, we'll just have to find it." He said. "Now go, go on." Santa waved the tiny elf away. Santa swung his legs out from under the covers.

"Oh dear." Mrs. Claus said, "You should stay in bed and rest."

"I probably should, my dear wife," Santa said standing up, "But I have to find my hat."

"I think Mrs. Claus is correct Santa." Dr. Coldhanz said. "You should definitely stay in bed and get some rest."

"Would if I could Doctor." Santa said. He looked around to make sure all of the little elves were out of the room. He even peaked under the bed just to make sure: those guys are not only little, but sneaky as well.

Quietly Santa said, "Mrs. Claus knows this Doctor, but you may not. It's impossible for me to deliver toys and goodies to the all the boys and girls of the world on Christmas Eve unless I am able to pause time. I can't pause time without my hat. It was a gift from Father Time a forever ago. It's to be used only during that special time when I race from sundown to sunrise on that one magic night." Santa paused and scratched his belly, "Besides, it's my favorite color: Red."

"But dear, we don't have any idea who stole it." Mrs. Claus said.

"I think I just might." He walked over to his wife and whispered in her ear; her eyes widened.

"Oh my!"

Three

Somewhere deep in the Blue Ice Mountains of the North Pole a small elf trudged through the falling snow. He was dressed head to toe in Elven Felt to keep warm, his pointy ears tucked nice and toasty into his felt cap. On his shoulders he carried a backpack.

It was early and still pretty dark out, so he had to go slow so as not get lost. Finally, he saw the mouth of the cave, his cave.

Iggy Blacknose stepped into the cave where it was much warmer than it was outside. Lighter too, as the cave walls were made of blue ice and had their own soft, pale, light. Iggy shrugged off his backpack and clapped his hands happily, dancing in a circle.

"I did it, I did it!" He chanted, a big smile on his face. His bushy eyebrows bounced up and down, and his eyes twinkled. He reached down, unzipped the backpack and pulled out a very soft, red hat. He twirled the hat around one finger then flung it into the air. As it came floating down,

he grabbed it and tossed it back up.

"He, he, he!" He cackled. "Now let's see you deliver all those presents! No presents, no Christmas. No Christmas, no more Christmas Elves! He, hah!" Iggy danced and laughed, "Phooey on all of you!" He did a cartwheel and landed with a plop on the floor.

For just one small moment a sad expression crossed Iggy's face. He thought of what might happen when Santa discovered the missing hat. He didn't want to hurt Santa's feelings. It was those mean elves, he thought. He wanted to get them for sure, but not Santa. He was always nice to me, Iggy thought. A tear slowly rolled down his cheek.

He sniffled and wiped his nose with his sleeve. Elves are not very neat and clean about stuff like that.

"Those elves, those mean, and... and... well, they're just mean!" Iggy said out loud.

Now Iggy Blacknose didn't always feel this way. Until just recently, he was as happy as any other elf. He was a handsome little guy with sharp, pointy ears, pointy feet, bushy hair, and a cute little white nose.

He liked nothing more than to sit all day in Christmas Castle making toys. Toy jet airplanes were his specialty. Then one day, not long ago, after taking a hot shower he was combing his hair when he noticed something odd about his nose. Why, there was a small black dot on the tippy tip! He tried to wash it off but that didn't work. He even used a scrub brush but nope, that didn't work either.

Iggy hoped the other elves wouldn't notice. And they didn't. Not that day. But the next morning after his hot shower Iggy looked in the mirror and nearly cried. The little black spot wasn't little anymore. It covered his whole nose! Can you imagine? Well, poor Iggy was in a panic. He didn't know what to do.

He tried covering it with whipped cream, but it tasted so good he kept licking it off. He was so embarrassed he didn't want to go to work. But he did.

You have likely already heard that the Christmas Elves love to make toys. They really do. There is something else that they love almost as much: to tease other elves! When they saw Iggy walk in that morning with a black nose they started laughing and laughing. Iggy's face turned as red as a Christmas tree ornament, but he went straight to work and tried to ignore the other elves.

"Hey! It's Iggy Blacknose." One shouted. "My name's Iggy Wiggler!" Iggy shouted back wiggling his ears, "See?"
And a few days later the teasing got worse.

"Iggy the black nose doesn't wear under clothes!" One of the elves yelled. Another said, "Little Iggy's weird and that's a fact, look at his nose all covered in black!" All the other elves started laughing.

Iggy couldn't take it anymore and ran out of the castle and back to his room. That night he slipped out of Christmas Castle. As he walked through the snow, he looked back at the castle all lit up with twinkling lights. His heart was as heavy as a bag of marbles and a tear rolled down his face.

"I'll be back someday," he said wiping away the tear, "And you'll be very, very sorry."

Iggy didn't stop walking until he made it to the Blue Ice Mountains. There he found a cave and made it his home.

A few days later, while Iggy was feeling very sorry for himself, an old man dressed all in white appeared at the mouth of the cave. The stranger explained to Iggy how he could get back at the elves and all their name-calling. He could get his revenge for all that they'd done to him. And that's just what Iggy did.

Four

Most kids know that on Christmas Eve Santa zooms around the earth in his big, red sleigh. He follows that magical hour just after bedtime and right before morning delivering toys and goodies. And I'm sure that you know how he does it. Santa is lucky enough to have living with him the world's only herd of flying reindeer. But guess what? Those reindeer are terrible pilots. Really. They have to go to flight school if they want to fly with Santa. And they all want to fly with Santa. Wouldn't you?

Now, not all of the reindeer pass flight school. Some end up staying home on Christmas Eve watching re-runs on television and eating popcorn.

As morning broke on the day-before-the-day-before-Christmas in the North Pole Santa made his way down to the flight line. He needed to talk to Dixon the flight instructor about getting a couple of his best students to help him rescue his hat.

Santa walked through the snow and as he came over a small hill, he saw the landing strip below. A few students were lined up at one end practicing their take-offs.

"Woah, look out below!" A small voice called from above. Santa looked up and quickly ducked as a small reindeer passed over his head. The flyer's legs stuck straight out in different directions and he spun slowly around and around.

"I can do it! I can do it!" The little deer said as he came in for a landing. Dixon stood at the end of the landing strip yelling directions.

"Straighten out! Slow down! Now...easy...come on Rupert...easy...pull up...gentle." The little reindeer glided in for a landing but at the last minute dropped with a plop and skidded across the snowy ground. "Look out!" Rupert shouted. Dixon scrambled to get out of the way, but it was too late. Rupert plowed right into him and they both slid across the ground and into a snowbank. Santa rushed down the hill to help. When he got there all he saw were eight furry reindeer legs sticking up out of the snow.

He pulled on a leg and out popped the little reindeer. Santa put him gently

on the ground. The little buck wobbled over to the rest of the group.

Dixon struggled out of the snow, stood, and shook his head. Snow fell from his large antlers. Santa looked at him and laughed.

"Ho, ho, ho! You'll need to be a little faster at getting out of the way next time old friend."

"Hmm," Dixon said, looking over at the young pilot. Rupert ducked behind one of his classmates. Dixon whispered to Santa, "This is the worst bunch of flyers I've ever seen."

"You say that every year, and yet every year you give me a great team." Santa said.

"We'll see Santa, we'll see." Dixon said.

Santa and Dixon walked toward the group of students.

"You've heard about my hat?" Santa asked quietly. Dixon stopped and looked at his boss.

"Everyone's heard Santa."

"Well, we need to go get it back. I'll be needing a couple of flyers." Dixon looked over at his students.

"Can I talk to you inside for a minute?" Dixon asked. He nodded his head in the direction of the snow cave that they use for a classroom. Santa nodded. Dixon turned to his students.

"I want all of you to practice your take-offs and landings. Especially you Rupert."

Santa and Dixon walked into the snow cave. This is where all the young deer come for ground school. Dixon had been teaching nearly forever it seemed and he'd had some pretty important students. On the walls around the classroom hung portraits of some of his most famous. Donner, Blitzen, Cupid, and Conner were all there, along with that one reindeer with the red nose.

What's his name? Yeah, you know his name. Dixon walked behind his desk and turned to Santa,

"Santa, I don't think any of these youngling's are ready."

"Oh, come now, surely you have at least a couple." Santa replied.

"I don't know Santa; I just don't know." Dixon looked at the ground, thinking. "I really need the next two days to get them ready for Christmas Eve. We still have to work on navigation, their take-offs are questionable, and you just saw how well they land."

Santa chuckled. "They will just have to do the best that they can. We have much to do and not much time in which to do it." Santa said, "Besides if we don't get my hat back, we won't have a Christmas Eve to worry about."

Dixon nodded. "Okay Santa, you're right. I'll see what I can do."

"That's the spirit!" Santa patted his old friend on the back, "I only need two, your two best."

"Only two?" Dixon asked.

"Yep, only two. You're coming with us."

"Me?" Dixon asked in shock. "But, but, but... I'm too old."

"Nonsense," Santa said, "I'm older than you are, and I'm going." Santa walked over to the mouth of the cave. "Out there is a sad and lonely little elf who has my hat. We're going to go and get it back."

Five

Santa stood next to his sleigh in the bright sunshine. This was not the one that he used for delivering the presents. That one was in the garage getting tuned up for the one-night dash across the planet. This one was his cruising sled. It looked a little like the big one but this one was much smaller. It was painted a bright red (of course) and had gold trim. The runners were made of polished diamonds slick as a wet seal and twice as fast. The seats were plump and comfy and two long leather straps rested on the front bar. Santa never really used the straps for much other than just hanging on. The reindeer usually knew where they were going.

"C'mon you guys," Santa said to a bunch of elves putting the reindeer in their harnesses, "Let's put a little jingle in it." He walked up to the reindeer. Dixon was up front with the two smaller deer, Bella and Rupert behind.

Santa could tell the two little deer were pretty nervous. He patted them on the back.

"Don't you guys worry about a thing, just follow the example of the old pro up front here and you'll be just fine."

"I'm not worried Santa." Bella said. She held her head high strutting against the harness. Rupert just gulped. He was really worried.

Santa climbed into the sleigh and grabbed ahold of the leather straps. The elves finished tightening the harness on the older deer. One gave Santa a thumbs-up sign as he jumped down.

"Okay Dixon, to the Blue Ice Mountains, Giddy ya!" And just like that the reindeer leaped into the sky. They snaked back and forth climbing higher and higher.

Santa looked back down at Christmas Castle growing smaller, and smaller. He wished he were back there right now. He'd probably be seated next to Mrs. Claus by the big fireplace eating a plate of cookies. He thought for a moment that he could smell the cookies baking. Wait a minute; he really could smell the cookies! Chocolate chip and walnuts! How could that be? He spied a wrapped-up bundle on the seat. A note tied to it twirled in the wind. The note read: I don't want you to lose any weight dear, Love, Mrs. Claus. Santa unwrapped the package. It was full of warm cookies.

"Ho, ho, ho!" Santa laughed and popped a cookie into his mouth. He scrunched up his eyebrows, gave the leather straps a shake and without spitting out any cookie crumbs shouted. "Come on you three, step on it. We've much to do and not much time in which to do it!"

Meanwhile, deep in the Blue Ice Mountains, Iggy was preparing for a journey of his own. He took the hat out of the backpack and carefully wrapped it in green paper. He put it back in and zipped up the pack. Next he walked over to his hiding spot and pulled out three magic jellybeans that the old man had given him: one red, one yellow, and the other green. He slipped his backpack onto his shoulders and walked to the mouth of the cave. He looked around and for just a moment felt very lonely. He thought back to his days at Christmas Castle. The days before his nose turned black. He missed making toys. He missed being with the other elves. Then he remembered how they'd teased him and how much it hurt inside. Still, I could take the hat back, he thought. I could put it back and then maybe go back to working in the castle. But he knew it was too late. He'd already done too much wrong.

So, before he could change his mind Iggy placed the three magical beans together in his hand: red, to yellow, to green. With a bright flash, a pale rainbow appeared out of the sky and Iggy stepped on board. Quickly he flew up and away from the Blue Ice Mountains. If he would have looked over his shoulder, he might have seen that far away a sleigh was coming. But Iggy was long gone by the time Santa and his reindeer landed at the base of the Blue Ice Mountains.

Santa poked his head into the cave from one side. Dixon did the same from the other, his antlers nearly poking Santa in the eye.

"Ahem." Santa said. Dixon rolled his eyes in Santa's direction.

"Oh, sorry Santa." He said and backed away.

Santa ducked his head and stepped into the cave.

"Iggy." He called, "Iggy Wiggler, come on out." His words echoed around the cave. But Iggy didn't come out. Santa searched the cave high and low. Nothing.

"Santa!" Dixon called from outside the cave. "We've found something!" Santa hustled outside. The reindeer were gathered around something in the snow.

"What is it?" He asked. Dixon pointed to the ground with a hoof. "Bella found it." The little deer raised her head proudly. "Good job Bella." Santa said. He bent down to look at the small object.

"Well wrap me in tinsel and call me a present." Santa said.

"What is it?" Rupert asked. Santa reached into the snow and picked up one bright, shiny green jellybean. He held it gently with two fingers. He looked at it first with one eye, then the other. Then he popped it into this mouth.

"Mmm, minty." He said.

"Santa what was it? What does it mean?" Bella asked.

"It means we still have a long way to go. Come on!"

Santa jumped into the sleigh and when the reindeer were back into their harnesses Santa yelled: "Giddy ya!" The reindeer leaped into the sky.

"Where are we going?" Rupert called out over his shoulder.

"To where the rainbows are born." Santa shouted, "Easter Valley!"

Six

Iggy sailed on the rainbow, over the pink and yellow mountains of the West and landed with a thumpody-thump on the spongy ground of Easter Valley. He bounced a couple of times and came to a stop right on a well-worn path next to a small pile of brown rocks. He sat up, looked around, and couldn't believe his eyes.

He was in a long, and deep valley with a small stream running right down the middle. The strange thing was that the water of the stream was bright purple. Not only that, everything else was all the wrong color too. On one side of the valley was a thick forest; the trees were bright reds and blues all jumbled together.

On the other side, a meadow of shiny white grass swayed in the gentle breeze. On both sides of the path on which Iggy sat grew groups of trees that had bright yellow bark with pink leaves shaped like stars.

"Amazing!" Iggy said. He got up and took off his backpack. He laid it on the pile of brown rocks. They felt soft and warm to the touch. Weird, Iggy thought. He broke off a small piece of rock and looked at it carefully. He sniffed the rock and thought it smelled familiar.

"Smells like chocolate." He said. He stuck out his little tongue and licked the rock. "It is chocolate!" He popped the whole piece in his mouth and chewed happily. Looking around a little more closely he noticed that some of the other things looked like they could be eaten too. Iggy ran over to the yellow trees. Standing up on his tippy-toes he popped off a pink star-leaf and without waiting to smell it, took a bite.

"Cotton Candy!" He exclaimed, "Incredible!"

It was then that he noticed the old man walking up the path between the trees. He was dressed all in white: A white coat with a pink flower in the pocket, white pants, white shoes, and even a white top hat with another pink flower tucked nicely in the hatband. Beside him trotted a very serious looking green, and yellow spotted dog.

Iggy swallowed the star-leaf with a gulp. There he is, he thought. The feelings of guilt over what he'd done were stronger than ever.

"Did you get it?" The man asked eagerly as he approached the elf. Iggy looked around to see if maybe the man was talking to someone else.

"Did I get what?"

"You know, the hat." The old man looked suspiciously at Iggy. "Well, did you get it?"

The man and dog stopped very close to Iggy, which made him a little nervous. And the man smelled kind of funny.

"Umm, yes, I did." He said and backed up a few steps.

"Good, good little elf." The man said breaking into a smile. His eyes lit up like fireworks. His bushy eyebrows went up and down like an out of control elevator. He stood there staring at Iggy for a few moments.

"Well, where is it?" He asked grumpily. Iggy glanced over to where his backpack sat on the pile of rocks. He was sure now that he didn't want to give away the hat. The old man saw where Iggy was looking.

"It's in the backpack eh?"

"Well," Iggy started, "Let me get it."

"That's okay." The old man said grabbing Iggy's little arm tightly. "I can get it." Iggy was amazed at how strong the old man was.

"No. Really," Iggy said, breaking free, "I can get it for you." He raced for the backpack. The green and yellow dog jumped in front of him growling and snarling. Black drool dripped from his mouth on to the path.

The old man chuckled. "I, or rather my dog Snoot here, would like you to let me get it." The old man walked over and picked up the backpack.

He unzipped it and pulled out the neatly wrapped green package. "You shouldn't leave something so valuable just lying around." He tossed the backpack over to Iggy. The old man's eyes sparkled as he gently held up the package.

"At last." He said in almost a whisper, "At last."

"What about what you promised me?" Iggy asked, "What about making my nose white again?" The old man looked up from the package. "Oh that," He said, "I can't actually do that."

"But you said!" Iggy cried.

"I know what I said foolish little elf. I had to say something, or you wouldn't have stolen the hat. I color eggs, not noses."

Just then from out of the sky a loud clatter of hooves could be heard.

"Giddy ya!" A voice called out. Iggy, the old man, and Snoot the dog, all looked up in amazement as Santa glided out of the sky and landed softly on the path. Quick as a wish Santa hopped out of the sled. Snoot the dog growled and the old man back up a few steps. He clutched the package tightly.

"Peter Cotton," Santa said as he approached, "What have you done?" The old man grabbed Iggy by the shoulder and took another step back. "Stay away Santa. You're too late, I've got it and it's mine."

"Now, now Peter. Don't do anything you'll regret later." Santa held out his hand and took another step closer and said firmly, "Give me back my hat."

Dixon, Rupert, and Bella struggled in their harnesses to free themselves, but they couldn't seem to get out. Rupert, being the smallest of the three, had the loosest harness. He struggled and struggled. He'd get one side loose and the other would tighten. It was no use. Seeing Rupert struggle, Bella grabbed one side of his harness with her mouth. She motioned for Rupert to work on the other side. Rupert nodded and started struggling once again.

"Santa it's over." The old man continued, "Your reign as the most loved Holiday Mystic is over. Without your hat you won't be able to pause time and there will be no more Christmas."

He let go of Iggy and held the package with one hand and finished untying the ribbon with the other.

"Now that I have this, I will be able to get around the world just as fast as I want. I will be the most loved Mystic." With that he ripped open the package.

"Peter no!" Santa shouted.

"It's mine! It's mine!" the old man, squealed with happiness. He threw the wrapping to the ground and felt the soft cloth in his hand.   His eyes grew wide as he stared at what he was holding. "What is this?" He shouted. In his hand, neatly folded, was a red and white, striped sock. Iggy turned to run from the old man, but he stepped on a piece of chocolate rock and tripped, falling flat.   His backpack flew out of his hands and spilled open.   And there on the ground lay the most famous hat in the entire world.

Seven

Old Peter Cotton stared at the hat. Santa stared at the hat. Iggy stared at the hat. In fact, everyone stared at the hat.

"You tricked me!" The old man shouted at Iggy. Iggy scrambled on all fours and reached for the hat. Just as his fingers touched the soft, warm wool Snoot the dog snatched it away with a growl.

"No!" Iggy yelled. He dove for the dog but just as he did Snoot snapped his head and flung the hat into the air toward the waiting arms of Peter Cotton. Santa reached up with both hands, but it was too high.

It was at that moment that Rupert broke free of his harness. With one giant step he leaped into the air. Flying over Peter Cotton's head, Rupert ducked, and Santa's hat fell neatly on his head right over his tiny antlers.

"No!" Peter cried.

All of a sudden everything seemed to pause. Iggy stopped in mid-dive for Snoot the dog, Santa stopped with his hands high in the air trying to catch the hat, and Peter Cotton stopped in the middle of saying no.

Everyone paused, as still as a snowman. Everyone that is except for Rupert who landed softly and trotted over to Santa. He lowered his head and Santa's hat fell to the ground at Santa's feet. And just like that everyone started up again.

"No...!" Peter continued.

Santa brought his hands down. He blinked and quickly spotting the hat on the ground, snatched it up.

"I...I...It was mine." Peter sobbed. "How could..."

Iggy backed away from the growling dog. He turned and bumped right into Santa. He quickly dropped his head and stared at the ground. He was so ashamed of what he'd done.

"Santa, I'm...I'm..." He couldn't finish. Santa gently rested his hand on the little elf's shoulder.

From out of the sky a loud clap of thunder shook the ground. A great wind blew from the North bending the trees. Pink star-leaves sailed away. Huge dark clouds rolled across the valley. A lightening bolt suddenly struck the ground and from the light stepped a very tall woman. She had flowing hair the color of rain; her eyes were as dark as the deep ocean. She was dressed in robes the color of the earth and in her hand, she held a very tall, snow-white staff.

"Mother Nature." Peter gasped; he shook with fright.

"Mother." Santa said and bowed his head. Iggy ducked behind Santa and hid behind his legs. There he found Rupert hiding as well. They both stuck their heads around and looked at the amazing woman.

"Peter Cotton," Mother Nature said in a voice like the sound of the wind. "What goes on here?" She walked over to the shaking old man.

"Tell me what you've done Peter."

Peter fell to the ground. "Oh Mother," he began, "I'm sorry. I'm sorry."

"I know Peter, I know. Tell me why? Why did you steal Santa's hat?"

Peter didn't answer for a moment. Finally, he whimpered quietly, "Because it's not fair." He looked over at Santa, "It's not fair that he is the most popular. It's not fair that the children love him the most. I work hard. I hide all of those beautiful eggs every year. But who loves me?"

"Peter, Peter, Peter," Mother Nature said, "Jealousy is a bad thing. A terrible thing." She moved toward Santa and looked at Iggy. "And revenge is just as terrible."

She turned once again and looked at Peter on his hands and knees.

"You let your jealousy grow so strong that you couldn't control it. Then you used a sad and bitter elf to help you. You have forgotten Peter. You have forgotten how happy you make the children Easter morning."

Peter sobbed quietly.

"No matter," Mother Nature continued, "I shall make you what you want: more...delightful."

With that she lifted her staff over her head and held it high.

A bright ray of light like the morning sun shot out of one end and touched Peter Cotton. In a flash the old man was no more. In his place hopped a very large, pure-white rabbit with a pink nose, and fluffy tail.

"You have your wish." Mother Nature said quietly. "You shall be even more loved than before. Faster too I should imagine." The rabbit sat up on its hind legs. A small smile spread across its face.

"Go forth and hide your eggs," Mother Nature said as the rabbit hopped away, "Peter Cotton-tail."

Snoot the dog, seeing the rabbit began to chase it. Mother Nature once again raised her staff and the light reached out and touched Snoot on the tip of his green and yellow tail. With a flash of light, the dog was gone. In his place sat a very plump squirrel. He twittered for a moment then ran lickety-split up the

nearest yellow tree. Mother Nature turned and looked toward Santa. Iggy ducked back behind his legs.

"Iggy Wiggler, come here!" Mother Nature called out. Santa stepped aside and Iggy and Rupert looked up at Mother Nature. Iggy bowed his head and approached the tall woman.

"You did what you did out of revenge." She said, "Because you were mad at being called names and teased by the other elves. You did it to get even."

Iggy nodded. Mother Nature continued, "Getting even with someone is never the answer, Iggy."

"I know." He mumbled.

"Be proud of who you are. Be proud to be different than the rest." She reached down and lifted his chin, looking him straight in the eyes, "I am." Mother Nature said.

"What's going to happen?" Iggy asked quietly. Mother Nature scratched her chin, and then smiled. "As your punishment you are to stay here. You are to help Peter Cottontail take care of Easter Valley where everything is beautiful. Beautiful, *because* it is different."

Iggy looked up, "Thank you Mother Nature." He said, and he hustled after the white rabbit.

Santa bowed his head in front of Mother Nature. "Mother Nature," He said, "Thank you."

"Of course, Santa, you're most welcome." She patted him on the shoulder. "Now, don't you have a lot to do?" She asked.

"And not much time in which to do it!" Santa answered. Mother Nature smiled, and with a clap of thunder she was gone.

Santa blinked and looked around. "Well," He said. "That was something." He looked down at Rupert who stood next to him. "Ready to go home my young reindeer?" He asked. Rupert nodded. They walked over to the sleigh and the other reindeer.

"Dixon my friend it's time for you to take a break." Dixon nodded, smiling. Santa unhitched him from the lead. "Rupert, Bella, up front." The two little reindeer couldn't believe what they were hearing. "You two lead us home." Santa said. The two young deer walked to the front of the sleigh. Rupert held his head high, no longer afraid. Santa hitched them up and then jumped into the sleigh.

"Giddy ya Rupert! Giddy ya Bella!" He shouted. "We have much to do, and not much time in which to do it!"

So that's how it happened as best as I can remember. Christmas came and went on schedule. Rupert became one of Santa's best flyers. And that's how Peter Cotton the old man became Peter Cottontail, the lovable, and quite fast, Easter Bunny. Bet you didn't know that!

I want to say thank you to some remarkable people: To Patricia Pettis, for never giving up on me, I love you Mom. To Colombina King, my muse, my motivation, my wife, te amo. To my friend and first editor, Deborah Hoppler, thank you Debs for the encouragement, the suggestions, and your friendship.

Made in the USA
Las Vegas, NV
15 December 2020